Diary of a Farting Creeper

Book 1: Why Does the Creeper Fart When He Should Explode?

An *Unofficial* Minecraft Book

By Wimpy Fart

Disclaimer and Terms of Use:

 Effort has been made to ensure that the information in this book is accurate and complete, however, the author and the publisher do not warrant the accuracy of the information, text and graphics contained within the book due to the rapidly changing nature of science, research, known and unknown facts and internet. The Author and the publisher do not hold any responsibility for errors, omissions or contrary interpretation of the subject matter herein. This book is presented solely for motivational and informational purposes only.

You're awesome for buying my book.

Check out other books by Wimpy Fart:

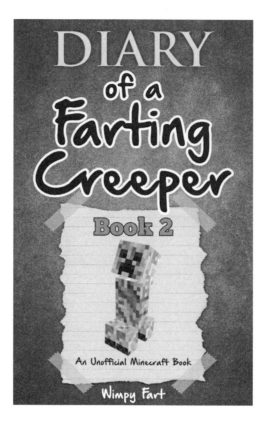

– Wimpy Fart –

Table of Contents

Wednesday

People at school called me names again. I'm having a hard time at school because the other creepers won't leave me alone. I wish they would all go away. This way I could just live my life. So what if I am the only creeper in Minecraft who can't explode? So what if I fart instead of blowing up? This is me!

I am already very sad and embarrassed, so people don't need to make life even more miserable for me. Don't they know creepers started as fart machines a long time ago — that's why we're green.

Every single day in school is a nightmare. To be honest, out of school is the same thing, because I live around the same people. My parents don't help at all! They just try to make me blow up, but I can't. All I do is fart and I have no idea how to change this.

Well, let me explain. We don't actually blow up; it just looks like we do. We actually make an explosion and we disappear. My little cousin already made his name known in the creeper community. He blew up when he met a human and he was just two years old. His parents are very proud of him, they always as my parents what's wrong with me. To make things worse, all my siblings have amazing blow up potential, even if none of them actually exploded until now. They can hiss really loud and if they focus, you can hear a small explosion, which means their body is ready to blow up.

All they need right now is a perfect moment to show off their explosion. My sister hunts every storm, trying to get herself charged, so she can make a bigger explosion when the time comes. I'm the only different one in my family.

Thursday

Another day at school, surrounded by creepers who can put up a decent explosion, while all I can do is fart...

I know that I am supposed to learn how to hiss and then explode, like all the good creepers, but I don't understand why everyone is so obsessed with it.

Even our neighbor, a skeleton, can make a huge explosion. My parents say he can do this because he's a skeleton and he has those long arms, which we don't. I don't understand how that works. Speaking of my parents, if they would have taken this blow up thing as serious as everyone days today then all my siblings and I wouldn't have been alive right now. They would've been too busy practicing explosions and probably not gotten married. That means my siblings and I would be...creeper dust!

Once I tried to ask our teacher, Miss Crunk, why can't we just hiss and move on, without blowing up but everyone laughed and mocked me. The only thing she said was that we need to practice a lot if we want to become decent creepers.

Problem is the more I try, the worse I am at this thing.

I remember the day when I found out I can't explode. It was the second week of school and we were given the instructions on how to hiss and we were supposed to expand our stomach's as big as we can so we could eventually blow up. Everyone in the class did it, but when it was my turn...

I walked in front of the class, smiling, I hissed and then tried to focus on pushing my stomach out when I heard this loud noise:

"BRRRRRRRRRRRRPPPPPPPPTTTTHH"

I farted really really loud. It sounded like fireworks!

Everyone laughed, but the teacher said these things happen, so I tried again.

The same result. I farted twice in front of the whole class. ☹

The teacher was really nice about it and she said I would be able to blow up at some point, but I just need to have more patience. After two months of non-stop farting I was the joke of the entire school and my parents were asked to come to school to talk to the teachers. The teacher told them I am "moist" and I won't be able to blow myself up. Like never.

My parents were sad, but they tried to find a cure for me. Nothing helps.

I am still the creeper who farts - most of the time it happens when I try to blow up but it also happens when I get nervous.

Today, for example, this creeper girl I like a lot was playing far away from the school when a human came to her and was pushing her around. She was scared so she just froze there and I went to her as soon as I could. I tried to stand up for her, but I was nervous so I farted and the human started to laugh at me. Really loud laugh, almost as loud as my fart, like he heard a great joke.

The girl punched me because my fart smelled really bad, she thought I farted on purpose so then she ran away. I just stood there while she ran away and the human laughed at me. I felt like such a loser! After a few minutes I found the strength to go back to my class, leaving the human alone. He was still rolling on the ground laughing.

So embarrassing!

Since that happened, everyone called me names like "stink bomb", "gas ball" or "fart knocker" because the only thing I can do is fart instead of blow up.

Friday

Today we learned more about cats and our teacher told us we should be afraid of them. I don't get it, why do we need to be afraid of them. I think they're creepy, but I want a specific reason... it's like being afraid of the dark.

I used to be afraid of the dark until I realized there was nothing in there to be afraid of, so I went on with my life. Same is the case with cats.

I asked the teacher what harm a cat can do to a creeper and her only response was that we don't know, but all creepers have been afraid of cats since the beginning of time.

I wish I could see a cat!

I don't even think is can hurt me – I mean come on, it's just a cat. They don't have weapons or armor or anything like that, like humans do. So, why are cats dangerous? I don't think they are.

After school I went to the library, trying to find out more about cats. All the books I read talk about how we are supposed to react when we see a cat — basically run away - but none of them say why we need to be afraid of cats.

Saturday

All the other creepers got together today to hang out: except me, of course. They say "stink bomb" isn't supposed to hang out with the real creeper kids. Sometimes creepers get together to find people to scare. Other creepers cut school and do it during the day sometimes too.

Sunday

My teacher called my parents and asked them to let me hang out with the other creepers. Apparently, our parents know we go out at day and roam the village and the mines, looking for someone to scare. It's always "They" and never "we", because I never join them.

I did go with them once and it was a mess. The group didn't know I was there, I stayed quiet because I didn't want them to see me and start making fun of me like they usually do. I just wanted to see how this "hang-out" thing works, so I was following. We got to the local village, where humans and villagers usually mind their own businesses. There are also two mines in the area, so plenty of human material to scared. I stayed close to the group, they were putting together some sort of plan. In a couple of minutes, two of the guys were on top of a house, while everyone else was on the ground. I could see where this was going and I wanted to watch, so I tried to get closer to them to have a better view. Suddenly, a villager showed up right in front of my face –I was shocked and scared and I ripped multiple farts! They were so loud FIRE came out of my butt.

Everyone saw what happened and they laughed so hard, that one of them almost blew up. No more sneaking around for me!

Now I am supposed to join the group for the next hang-out, which is scheduled next week. Yuck! The thought of spending time with those guys makes me... fart. Yes, I am standing here, farting, instead of blowing up. Not even a small explosion! Nothing!

Monday

Today we have my favorite class: soccer! I am the king of soccer!

No one can beat me at this game, even if they can beat me at everything else, especially blowing up. On the soccer field I can hit the ball like no other creeper and this is why all the other boys in the class want me on their team. The girls like watching me play soccer too, including Addison: she stands in the front row and watches every move I make. Sometimes I think she likes me.

When the soccer class was over and we all went to the mobbing class, a horrific stench surrounded us. Everyone thought it was me again. The teacher decided to send me outside so I wouldn't disturb the class. It was fine, I needed a break anyway. When I went outside I ran into Spike. Spike is a zombie – the bad smelling type of zombie. When Spike is in the area you can smell him from about 6 blocks away.

The poor guy is probably one of the most generous and warm-hearted zombies that has ever spawned in Minecraft. I once saw him help a skeleton gather his severed limbs, which is not something any random zombie would do. Most of them, if not all, except Spike, just roam around the villages and attack humans as well as villagers. But not Spike.

We said hi to each other and then minded our own businesses around the school. I realized we were just in front of my class, so the smell wasn't from my farts, but from Spike.

Tuesday

Okay, now I am really mad at the creepers!

Today I was eating my lunch in the cafeteria, while a group of young creepers were sitting in a group listening to one of them telling stories. I was eating my food, and listening to what they were saying since I was right next to them. Suddenly, someone farted. Not me! I swear! Not me!

The entire group turned around and looked at me. Someone said "Stink Bomb did it!" Another creeper, who was eating next to me, a couple of tables to the right, jumped on the table and started to sing "Beans, beans, good for butt; the more you eat, the more you fart!"

This started a food fight and soon everyone was singing this stupid song, jumping around and throwing food at me. I got really angry and started to hiss uncontrollably, then I ripped a really powerful fart, so powerful I lifted 3 feet off the ground. It was like a small explosion – which gave me some hope to be honest! And definitely the longest, loudest fart I've ever produced in my short life.

This scared everyone so it ended the food fight, I didn't know what to do so I just ran away from school and walked around the neighborhood until it was time to go home. I will never go back to school!

Wednesday

It was time to go to school and I had no idea what to do this morning. I went to my parents and told them I won't go to school anymore, but they didn't agree, so I needed to go to school again. Pff!

As I was walking to school I saw something in the hills, just next to the road. I went over to check what was there and when I got close I saw a pack of cats trying to hunt a skeleton. The guy was clearly in trouble and I didn't mind a detour, so I went over to try and help him, hissing as loud as I could.

When I approached I saw the cats were in fact wolves. The wolves weren't impressed with my hissing and one of them jumped in front of me and tried bite me. I avoided it by a split second, but then five wolves surrounded me, while three were trying to bite the skeleton. I tried to kick them, like I do when I play soccer, but they kept attacking me. The situation was not good at all!

But suddenly I remembered what happened yesterday in the cafeteria, so I tried and I pushed my stomach really hard and did what I do best: I farted!

BBRRRRUUPPPPTH!

The entire pack backed off a little, looking confused. The skeleton asked me to do it again, and I did:

BBBEEEEERRRRPPPPPPPPPPPPTTTTH

All of a sudden the wolves got scared and turned around. The skeleton shot a couple of arrows at them and they ran away.

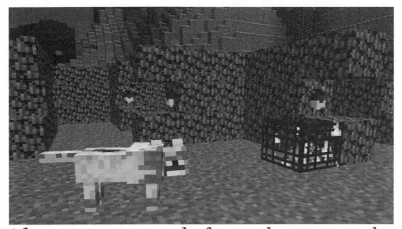

After we recovered from the scare, the skeleton was really impressed by my super-power which scared off the wolves. His name is Steve and he got lost while trying to hunt a human. Then one wolf got his track and before he knew it, he was surrounded by an entire pack.

He was really happy that I stopped by to save him, so he invited me to his house. I told him I can't go, but planned to meet him the next day, in the same place to talk some more.

At school the teacher was talking about cats, which reminded me of my own questions. If cats are similar to dogs and they come from wild cats and dogs, how comes wolves got scared of my fart? I was supposed to be scared of them, right?

The entire day I was haunted by this thought...

Thursday

I was so excited to meet Steve again and as soon as I woke up I grabbed my things and headed straight to the woods, where he was waiting for me. When I got there I saw he had company: a zombie.

"Hey, dude! This is LJ, my friend. I hope you don't mind he's here. When he heard about your powers, he wanted to meet you."

"No, no problem, I am happy to meet you LJ."

"So, how are you?"

"Fine, thanks..."

"I know this is short, but can you do us a favor?"

"What?"

"Yesterday you farted and scared off wolves..."

"Yup!"

"Can you do it again?"

"I think so... I mean, I can fart, and people always make fun of me and call me names"

"They make fun of you and call you names?"

"Yes, because of my... you know... farts!"

"So What? Why is that?"

"As creepers we are supposed to blow up, not fart. So when I hiss I should be exploding right after. But I can't! I can only come up with a loud smelly fart, so people call me Stink Bomb."

"Hey, but that sounds dangerous....if you make an explosion can you get hurt?"

"Only creepers can do it, we don't hurt because we're creepers so we disappear. But humans and other animals would get hurt if they tried."

"That's strange!"

"Anyway, let's get to the point, here! I know it's a lot to ask, because we've just met, but we need your help."

"You need my help? I think I've crossed the Minecraft realm and landed in a fantasy game!"

"Come on! Just because your friends at school call you names and don't appreciate you, doesn't mean everyone in the world will make fun of you!"

"They're not his friends, Steve. Friends like each other and appreciate each other."

"Guys, can we get to the point here?"

"Oh, yea! Here's the problem: we all live underground, just below a village. This was perfect until couple of months ago, when a human showed up in the village, trading and doing stuff. Then, a whole bunch of them showed up!"

"But you go out at at night, when humans sleep!"

"We do go out at night, but humans don't sleep! They brought a lot of torches with them and lately they have cats and dogs. Last week the chief of the Skeleton Commission was chased by the dogs and those humans decided to get rid of us. They used the dogs to sniff our small city and they are planning a huge attack."

"The attack is going to take place this weekend!"

"So how can I help you?"

"You can scare dogs!"

"I think so..."

"If we can get rid of dogs we can fight the humans and stay alive. But if the dogs reach us before the humans, they weaken our forces. Bottom line is, we need your help!"

"I don't know what to say..."

"Yes would be a great answer."

"Then... yes?"

"Great! Come on, we have to announce the other mobs!"

"Wait! Steve! How am I supposed to help you?"

"Our spies will find the exact time of the human attack and you have to be with us on that day. When a dog approaches, you fart, to scare it off."

"And cats? Does it work on cats too?"

"I don't know, LJ."

"Can't we find out?"

"Cats don't even live here; they are only in the jungle."

"There's one around the witch's house, in the swamp."

"Let's go to the swamp and find out if I can scare cats, then!"

"I will go with you; LJ, go home and let everyone know about our plan!"

"Ok, bye!"

I was thrilled – finally I'll get to see a cat at last! It was like a dream come true. When we reached the swamp, I saw the witch's hut towering above the ground, but there was no cat around. Steve shot a fish with his bow and we placed it as bait, then we sat behind a bush, waiting for the cat.

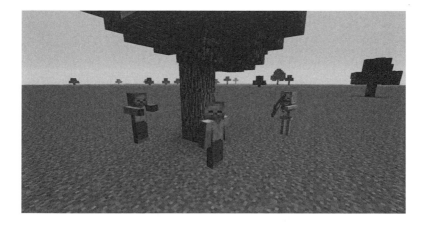

We waited a lot, and then finally, our patience paid off: a cat showed up, he smelled the fish. I gathered all my courage and stepped out. The cat looked up at me. I started to hiss. It started to hiss as well. Then, the cat moved towards me, slowly. When it was a couple of inches from my legs I farted. Loud and clear as always, especially because I've been keeping this one fart for a lot of time.

And it had the perfect result! The cat jumped backwards, and then it ran away!

Awesome!

I was the only creeper who was not afraid of cats! Cats would run away from my farts!

"Way to go! Hooray!"

"Did you see that?"

"Of course I did! Now let's go home; we have to plan the attack and you need to save some farts for the big day!"

I went home in a really happy mood. I was so happy and excited my parents were wondering what happened. But I didn't tell them. I wanted to surprise them when the time is right.

Friday

Today I met up with Steve again and he told me the fight is going to be on Sunday. I can't wait for it to happen! He also told me that I need to see their Ender, who is the mob city's doctor. The Ender worried that my farts could be a symptom of a disease or something, so I agreed.

Steve took me to a large field where there was a Nether portal towering next to a small house. The house was the Ender's lab, as he was also a sort of guardian for the portal.

"Hello Steve!"

"Hello, Doc! Here is the creeper I told you about."

"Oh, sure, the one who farts?"

"Yup, the one who farts"...

"So, when do you fart?"

"Umm..."

"Stop worrying! Spell it out!"

"When everyone at school practices hissing and expanding so they can blow up a little, I fart."

"Aha! So it's after the hiss?"

"Yes."

"Let me check your charge."

The Doc scanned me with a strange device, which apparently did nothing.

"My boy, you don't have the right gas mix."

"What? What's that?"

"Don't they teach you what makes you explode?"

"No! They just tell us how to do it."

"Where is the mob schooling system going these days? My boy, creepers blow themselves up because they have their bellies filled with gases. The vibrations from the hissing make the gases explode."

"Why can't I explode?"

"You have a different mix of gases. To be more precise, your body lacks one of the gases, so the hissing doesn't produce an explosion, but a gas discharge."

"What does this mean?"

"You are healthy and you can do whatever a creeper does, but you can't blow up."

"I see..."

The visit made me happy, because now I knew what was wrong with me. The only thing that confused me was what caused the different gas mixture in my body. The Doc told me I won't be able to do anything, so eating or drinking something to make up for that gas was not possible.

So in a nutshell, I was going to be "the one that farts" all my life. Hah! At least now I know how to use my fart power to scare cats and help people in trouble...

Saturday

I am so excited for the big fight! I want to go to sleep and wake up tomorrow!!!

But before that, I have a mission: I need to control learn to control my farts. If I am going to fart on demand, I need to hold the gas and release loud bombs when I want to. I'm going to practice for a while then I'm going to bed. My Sunday is going to be awesome. Way more fun than hanging out with the other creepers! Who needs them anyway!

Sunday

The big day had come!!!

I was so excited that I felt some strange bubbling in my stomach and thought I was going to explode, but it turned out I was just cooking a huge fart in my stomach. I told my parents that I was going to hang out with some creepers from school, but I actually met Steve and LJ. They took me to where they live, which is really different from my creeper community!

These guys had an entire city underground. When I walked through those large gates, I saw tons of skeletons and zombies roaming around. A couple of spiders were placing webs on the cave ceilings. However, there was no creeper in this huge metropolis. As I was looking all around me, a spider came to Steve and told him the humans are getting ready.

"Come on, if we win the fight, you will have all the time in the world to stare at the buildings!"

We walked to a mine-cart and rode it towards a large cave, where there was a small army of skeletons and zombies - about 20 mobs, all of them really anxious. Steve told me they were expecting the humans to come. The plan was simple: I was the one who was going to be in the front line, meeting the dogs. Steve and LJ were going to be with me, making sure I don't get hurt. And when the dogs run away, the other mobs were going to take care of the humans.

Depending on how many humans were going to flood the cave, there was another way to put off their dogs. The cave was lined with bridges, each of which was packed with a loud speaker system that could transform any sneeze into a loud noise. I tried it out, squeezing out a small fart, which sounded like the biggest thunder ever. If that was not going to scare the dogs, nothing was going to do it!

The cave had two tunnels, and we used one of them to get inside; the other one being the one used by humans because it opened in the village above us.

The spider came running towards us, yelling that the fight was about to start. I was ready!

The first thing I saw was a human, all dressed up in armor, surrounded by cats. There were cats, not dogs, but this didn't scare me at all. LJ and Steve took care of the human, but once they shot him, a dog came out of nowhere and attacked them. I went to them and distracted the dog and then farted as loud as I could. To everyone's delight, the cats jumped backwards and ran away, while the dog froze for a second then backed off. Nice, this was only the beginning!

Steve took me inside a large cage, on the bridge, from there we could see the fight underneath us and spot any dogs if they showed up. The speaker system was ready to make each fart into a huge thunder-fart.

The fight was going really good for us: the skeletons were shooting the humans from a distance, while the zombies and the spiders attacked them one by one.

"There's a dog!"

"Oh, yeah..."

Because there was only one dog so far, I released a small fart, which sounded 10 time louder, thanks to the speaker system. The dog ran away, just like I knew he would.

After one minute an entire pack of about 20 dogs showed up, so it was time for a big one, the real deal. I pushed and farted as hard as I could. I'm not sure what happened but I accidentally released a really bad smell, it almost made the humans faint! I guess that's why they gave up on the fight five minutes later, they ran away and some of them were throwing up.

Mission accomplished!

When the last human was chased out of the mob city everyone cheered and wanted to thank me. It turned into a party, which ended really late. I was the hero!

When I got home my parents were waiting for me. They were really upset; really, really upset. I don't think I ever saw them this upset ever before. I told them where I was and what I did, but they weren't happy about me talking to strangers and stuff.

Monday

I had another serious talk with my parents and they agreed to meet Steve and LJ. They were happy to hear that I put my farting power to good use.

When I got to school today everyone heard about the fight and now some creepers want to be my friend. A few of them even want me to teach them how to fart!

Steve just called. He said the humans were planning a bigger fight – so there was a huge battle coming up and he needs me to teach everyone how to fart so we can counter them.

What have I started? This is going to be crazy!

Book 2 is available on Amazon.com

– Wimpy Fart –